THE PRINCE OF EGYP

Miriam's Gift

DREAMWORKS

In the land of Egypt, there lived a Hebrew family—a mother, a father, and two young children. They were slaves and so their lives were very hard. Every day they were forced to work, even the children. They helped build great temples and monuments for the ruler of the land, the Pharaoh. At night they returned home exhausted and hungry. But this family found comfort in one another, and in their faith that one day they would be set free.

When a new baby boy was born, they were overjoyed, especially the little girl, Miriam. She knew that this baby was special. As she cradled him in her arms, she thought, *Little brother, I will always take care of you. And I have a feeling that someday you will help me, too.*

But she worried about her brother.

Pharaoh had decided that the Hebrew slaves were growing too numerous and strong. No new baby boy was safe from Pharaoh's men. Miriam's mother, Yocheved, said to her children, "Miriam, Aaron, we must take your brother away from here to keep him safe."

Miriam loved the baby dearly. She did not want him to leave their home, but she understood that his life depended on it. She followed her mother down to the river. Yocheved put her little son in a snug basket and prayed that the river would bring it to safety.

She softly sang a last lullaby to her son, *"Hush now, my baby, be still, love, don't cry."* She placed the basket on the water's surface, singing, *"River, O River, flow gently for me, such precious cargo you bear. Do you know somewhere he can live free? River, deliver him there."*

To make sure the baby was safe, Miriam followed
the basket as it bobbed and floated down the river. She
watched, frightened, as the crocodile snapped its jaws,
the hippo gnashed its teeth, and the fishermen cast their
nets. But the basket floated past each danger. Miriam
believed God was watching over the basket, too.

She thought, *Do not worry, brother. I won't leave you
until you are safe.*

But just when Miriam believed the little boat
was out of harm's way, it drifted straight toward the
Pharaoh's palace!

She watched as the basket glided across the river into a tranquil water garden where women of the court were bathing. Miriam almost cried out when she saw the Queen wade to the basket and slowly lift the lid...but to the little girl's relief, the Queen smiled.

Miriam thought, *Brother, you're safe now, and safe may you stay. For I have a prayer just for you: Grow, baby brother. Come back someday. Come and deliver us, too.*

The Queen held the baby tenderly, turned to her own young son, and said, "Come, Rameses, we will show Pharaoh your new baby brother. We will call him Moses."

Before Miriam went home, she weaved a stalk of bulrush into the shape of a basket. She thought, *I will hang this around my neck to keep Moses close to my heart. It will remind me of my faith that God will answer my prayer.*

As the years passed, Miriam and her brother Aaron learned to work very hard, but they hated the cruel way the Egyptians treated their people.

One day, as Miriam was carrying water to other slaves, she heard a guard yell, "Move faster!"

A slave fell.

"Get up, old man!" yelled the guard. And he threatened the frightened man with his whip.

"Stop it!" Miriam shouted. She quickly helped the slave sit up and gave him water to drink. Such kindness and courage made Miriam a leader among her people.

She often saw Moses, now big and strong, with Prince Rameses. They rode by in chariots, shouting and laughing. Once, they destroyed a temple that the slaves had just built, but rode off without even glancing back.

Miriam thought, *The slaves don't like Moses. It's easy to see why. But I must have faith that someday he will help set us free. I know it. Although each day of work makes it harder to believe.*

Life was very difficult. One day, Aaron and Miriam came home tired to the point of despair. As Aaron drew water from a well, Miriam sat staring at the ground. Aaron watched her and worried. He, like everyone, relied on Miriam's strength and good spirits. It frightened him to see her look so discouraged.

Miriam sighed to herself, thinking, *Each new day of work is hard to face, but I have to believe that God is listening to our pleas.*

Suddenly, she looked up and noticed a young man walking toward her. It was Moses! *God has brought him to our very door!* Miriam thought. But Moses was looking elsewhere, not at her.

Miriam was so surprised to see him, she stammered, "Oh! Oh–oh–my brother! You are...here of all places...at our door...at last!"

"What?" Moses said, equally surprised.

Miriam touched his arm, but he jerked away.

"Miriam, please..." Aaron whispered, worried that she might anger the prince and be punished.

Miriam would not listen. "Moses, you are not a prince of Egypt. You are our brother. You must believe!"

"Enough of this!" shouted Moses. He was amazed that a slave girl would dare to talk to him this way.

"She is confused and knows not to whom she speaks," said Aaron to Moses as he picked up Miriam by the waist and tried to carry her into the house.

"No, Aaron!" cried Miriam. She broke free and ran to Moses. "Our mother set you adrift in a basket to save your life," she said.

Moses just stared at her. He still did not remember. "Save my life? From whom?"

"Ask the man you call Father!" Miriam replied bitterly.

"How dare you!" shouted Moses, enraged.

Moses! Miriam thought, *I am your sister. If only I could make you remember!*

Miriam dropped to her knees and began to sing their mother's lullaby:

> *Hush now, my baby,*
> *Be still, love, don't cry.*
> *Sleep as you're rocked*
> *By the stream,*
> *Sleep and remember*
> *My last lullaby,*
> *So I'll be with you*
> *When you dream.*

A strange look crossed Moses' face, but then he turned suddenly, and ran away. And he did not come back for a long time.

Many years went by, but Miriam was sure Moses would return. She was so certain that she told the entire slave village about her belief that Moses would help them. "Rejoice! My brother Moses is going to come back and help us escape this slavery!"

"Oh, Miriam! You and your crazy dreams!" Her neighbor laughed. "Do you really believe a prince of Egypt is related to you?"

"Yes, he's my brother. He will help set us free, you'll see!"

"But Miriam, if Prince Moses is our deliverer, then why doesn't he return to us?" one woman asked. The villagers had heard that he had left Egypt for good and gone to live in the desert.

Miriam wondered, *Moses, where are you? I just know you will come back, but when?*

It had been many years since the slaves saw Moses. One day, as Miriam walked with Aaron by Pharaoh's palace, she noticed a gathering of people in the distance. The crowd circled around a shepherd.

"It is Moses!" a woman said to Miriam. "I've heard that he has been to see Rameses, our new Pharaoh. Moses told him that God commands Pharaoh to set us free. Do you think he has gone mad?"

When Miriam heard her brother's name, her heart beat very fast. She ran closer to the crowd.

"Well, of course, Pharaoh was furious," the woman continued, hurrying to keep up. "He said he would not let us go, but double our workload instead! And it's all Moses' fault!"

"You are no help to us," the slaves were yelling at Moses. "Go away!" They threw mud and stones at him. Aaron joined the crowd.

Moses looked ready to give up. But Miriam was angry at the slaves, especially Aaron. "You shame yourselves!" she yelled at them, and they were silent. She held out her hand to Moses, who looked relieved to see her. "I have faith in you, Moses. God has guided you back here. God will not abandon you. So don't you abandon us."

With Miriam at his side, Moses walked down to the Nile, where Rameses reclined in his luxurious barge.

"God commands that you let His people go!" Moses yelled from the bank.

"Commands?" Rameses laughed. "I will never let them go!"

"Then behold, the power of God!" Moses shouted. The slaves gathered to watch as he placed his shepherd's staff into the great Nile River. Rameses' soldiers screamed in terror. The water had turned to blood.

Moses turned back to the slaves and said, "Pharaoh has the power. He can take away your food. He can even take away your lives. But there is one thing he cannot take away. Your faith. Believe–for we will see God's wonders."

Miriam was amazed at what she was seeing. *Perhaps I am dreaming,* she thought. But when she looked at the river again, it was still blood. *Our God is real! But if this is the strength of God's power, dreadful things may happen because of Pharaoh's stubbornness.*

And dreadful things did follow. The Egyptians' water and food became polluted. The land and sky darkened with frogs, insects, and hail. Animals died. Boils appeared on the skin of people and beasts. And the sunlight dimmed to a blackness so thick that it could be felt. But Rameses refused to free the slaves.

Finally, Moses warned Rameses of a last, most devastating plague. But Rameses *still* would not let the slaves go.

So Moses told the Hebrews of God's plan. "Mark every door with lamb's blood. Tonight the Plague of Death will visit every firstborn son, but if you have a mark of blood upon your door, the plague will not enter."

Miriam comforted the children and helped her neighbors get ready for the night. "Everything will be fine. We are in God's hands," she said.

During the long night, Rameses lost his son, the last of all he cherished. In despair, he gave the slaves permission to leave.

Miriam awoke from a troubled sleep to join the Hebrews pouring out of their homes. They began their long journey out of Egypt.

They stopped at the shore of the Red Sea. How could they cross it? And worse, the Egyptian army was not far behind. Calling upon God's powers, Moses planted his staff in the sea and two great walls of water surged up to reveal a winding pathway.

Moses and Miriam led the Hebrews through the narrow path. "Hurry! Hurry!" the running people shouted. Just as the last of them reached the other side, the walls crashed down on the advancing soldiers.

Moses approached his sister, who he realized had given him a great gift–her faith. "Thank you," he said. Miriam smiled at her brother. Finally, she could look toward their future with joy. *Today is my first day of freedom. There can be miracles when you believe.*

A Faith Journal

Miriam always had faith in Moses' mission no matter what others thought. Here is a journal for you to record your beliefs about other people and yourself.

Share your ideas of what it means to be a good brother or sister.

_____

_____

_____

What is the nicest thing you have done recently for someone in your family?

_____

_____

_____

_____

What does faith mean to you? Who teaches you faith? How?

_____

_____

_____

_____

_____